SCOUT

AND THE

TANK

Bailey Whitlock

This book belongs to:

____

Good Morning!
?
Good Afternoon!
?
Good Evening!
?

Scout said hello to all the other fish. No one would say hi back.

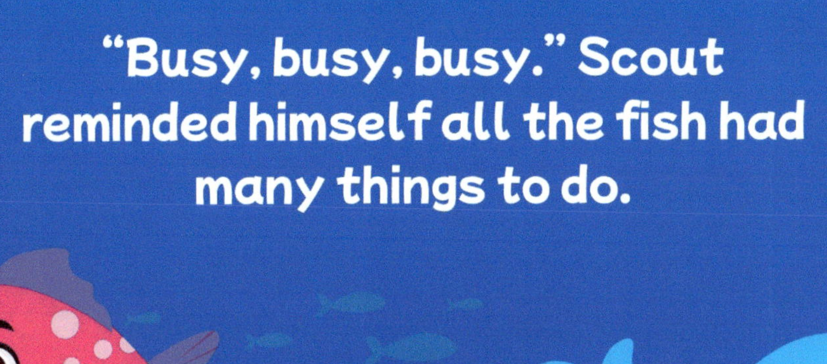

"Busy, busy, busy." Scout
reminded himself all the fish had
many things to do.

"Woohoo! A new day! Let's go say hello," Scout said this every morning. He didn't know today would be a very different day.

Scout swam his normal route. He noticed something odd. He stopped swimming. All the other fish ran right into him. It was a traffic jam!

Two humans stared at Scout. "How can this be?" Humans were only in story books Scout's mom read to him when he was a baby fish.

Scout followed them up and down the window. What he saw amazed him. "They look so kind. Wow! They waved back at me. I must tell the other fish!"

Frantically, Scout swam back and forth to tell the other fish. No one listened to Scout.

How did they not see those humans? They were right there, Scout thought.

Scout went home
very sad.

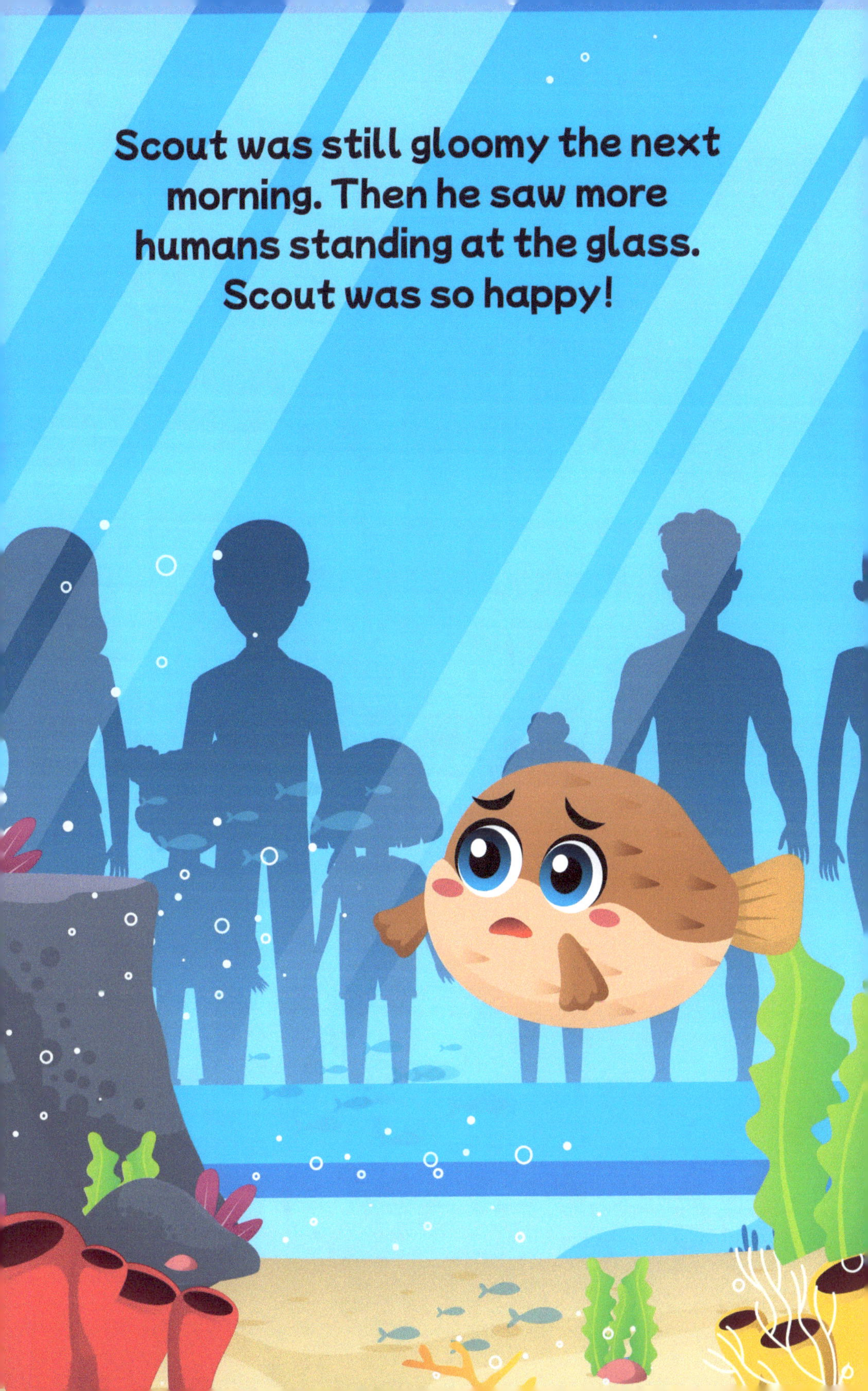

Scout was still gloomy the next morning. Then he saw more humans standing at the glass. Scout was so happy!

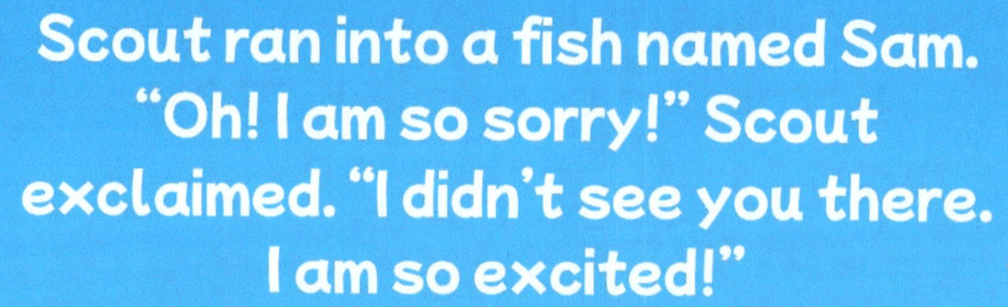

Scout ran into a fish named Sam.
"Oh! I am so sorry!" Scout
exclaimed. "I didn't see you there.
I am so excited!"

Scout knocked Sam out of the swim path. Sam looked around. . He was excited by Scout's news.

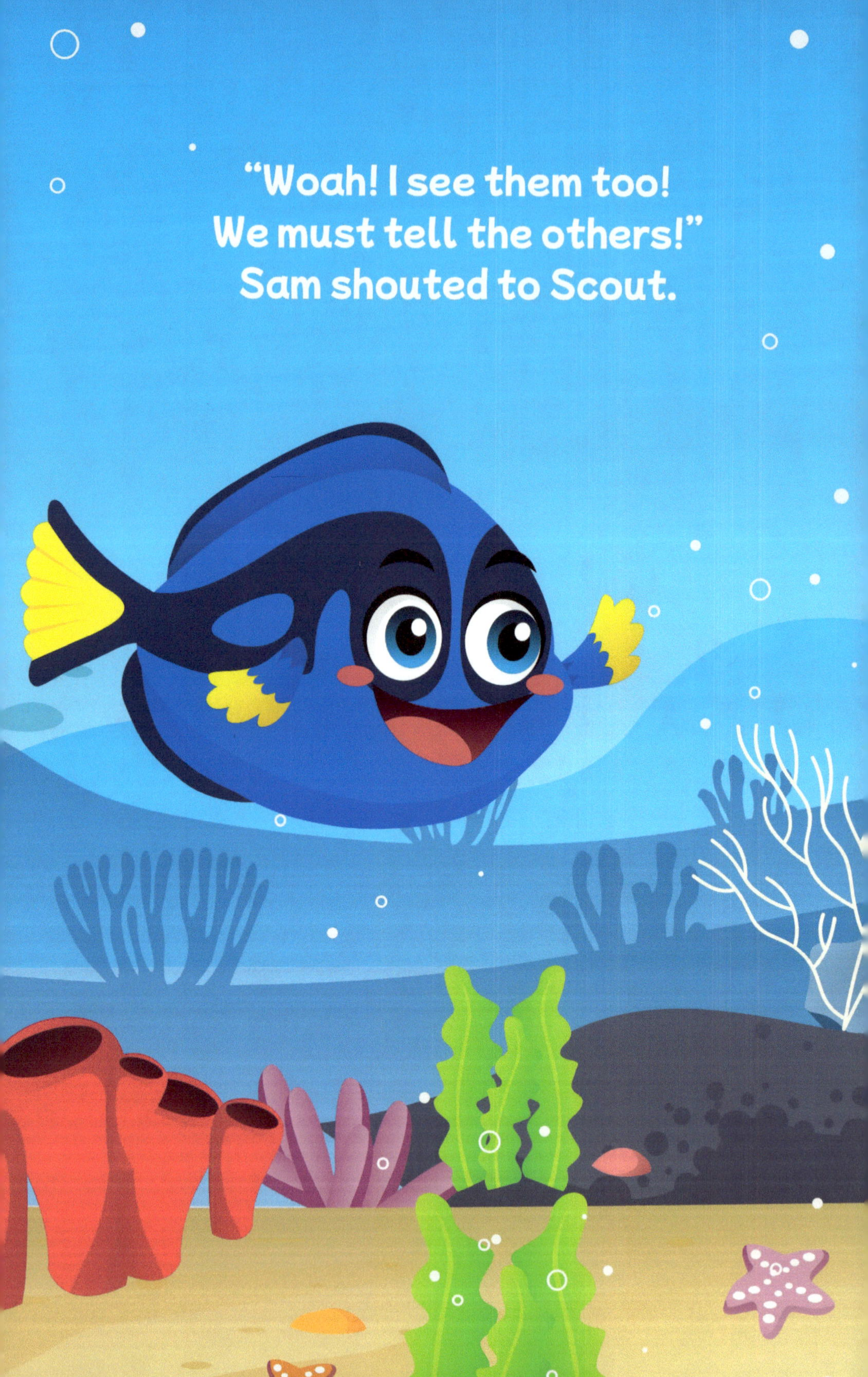
"Woah! I see them too!
We must tell the others!"
Sam shouted to Scout.

Scout and Sam came up with a game plan. They would stop all of the fish. The others would listen to what they said.
PLAN

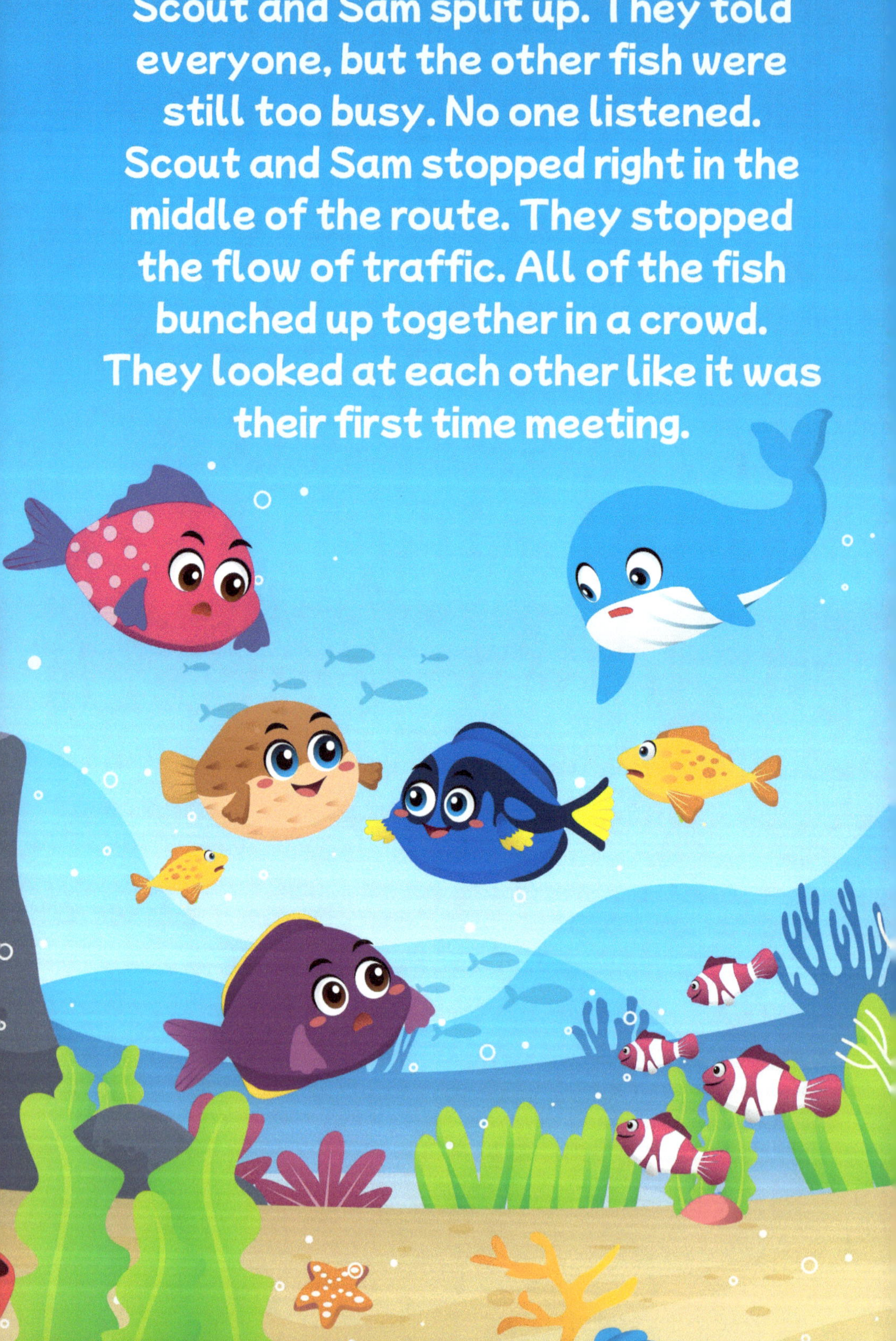

Scout and Sam split up. They told everyone, but the other fish were still too busy. No one listened. Scout and Sam stopped right in the middle of the route. They stopped the flow of traffic. All of the fish bunched up together in a crowd. They looked at each other like it was their first time meeting.

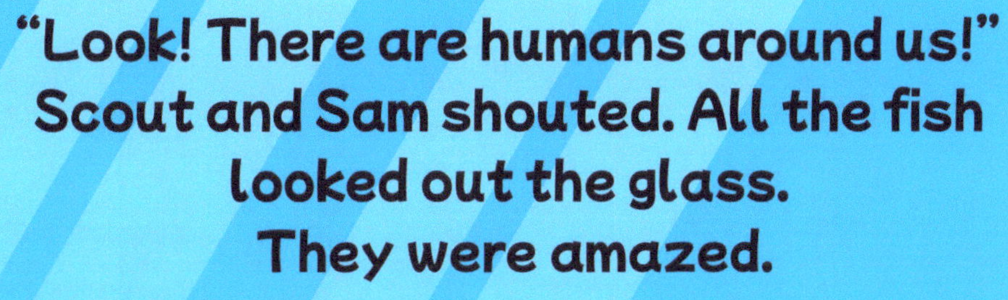

"Look! There are humans around us!"
Scout and Sam shouted. All the fish
looked out the glass.
They were amazed.

"Wow. How did we not
notice where we live?"
One fish exclaimed. "We are around
this every day."

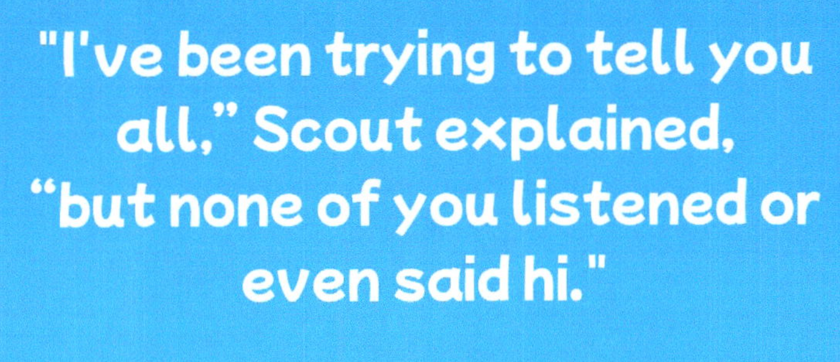
"I've been trying to tell you all," Scout explained, "but none of you listened or even said hi."

The crowd of fish realized how mean they had been to Scout. They told him they were sorry.

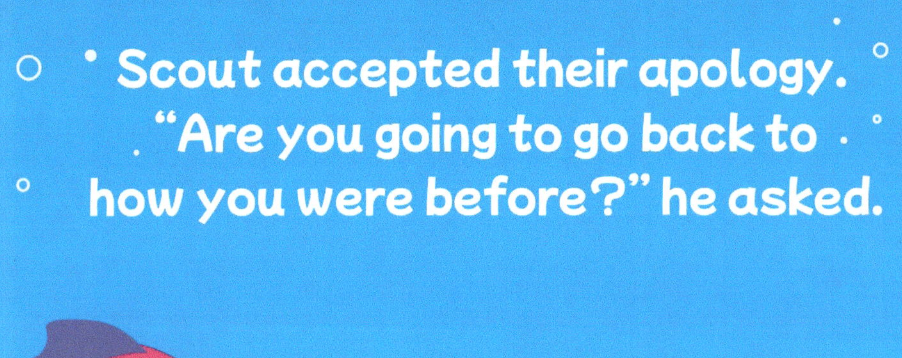
Scout accepted their apology.
"Are you going to go back to
how you were before?" he asked.

"We do not know how else to live,"
the fish replied.

Scout and Sam went home that night. They were very sad and defeated. "At least we tried," Sam said."Yeah, thanks for your help," Scout replied.

The next morning, Scout and Sam started their day. They heard voices and laughter. They were happy to see the other fish enjoying each other's company.

The community gathered in a circle around Scout and Sam. "Thank you for showing us a new way to live," they said. "We were so busy we didn't care about what happened around us. We missed out on love and friendship for so long. That changes today!"
"Thank you, Scout and Sam!"

Good Morning!
Good Morning Scout!
Good Afternoon!
Good Afternoon Scout!
Good Evening!
Good Evening Scout!

THE END